Date Due

NOV 16 1972	JY 8 '80	
MAR 10 1973	DE 27 '80	
	AG 4 '81	
MAY 8 1973	DE 8 '81	
JUN 14 1973	JA 16 '82	
JUN 28 1973	MY 4 '82	
OCT 21 1975	JY 16 '82	
APR 9 '77	SEPT. 7 1982 OCT. 2 1982	
NOV 26 '77		
AUG 3 '78		
JY 21 '81		

141

GREGORY GRAY
and the
BRAVE BEAST

By Mary Collins Dunne

Illustrated by Lois Axeman

 CHILDRENS PRESS, CHICAGO

141

For my daughter, Christine

Library of Congress Cataloging in Publication Data

Dunne, Mary Collins.
  Gregory Gray and the brave beast.

  SUMMARY: A lonely six-year-old boy makes friends
with a tomcat.
  [1. Stories in rhyme. 2. Pets—Stories]
I. Axeman, Lois, illus. II. Title.
PZ8.3.D926Gr   398′ .8 [E]   72-1462
ISBN 0-516-03467-7

Library of Congress Catalog Card Number: 72-1462

1 2 3 4 5 6 7 8 9 10 11 12 13 14 15 16 17 18 19 20 21 22 23 24 25 R 75 74 73 72

On the steepest of the city's hills
Stood a big old house with fancy sills,
Balconies, towers, gingerbread trim,
Stairways curving and hallways dim.

When long ago it was new and fine,
Famous people came to dine.
    Each week a score
    Passed through the door
As carriages stopped to let out more.

But the walls rang now
   With a different noise,
For the house was
   A boarding school
      For boys.

In June the boys left for vacations
Which they all spent with their relations.
　　But Gregory Gray
　　Had to stay.
His parents were traveling far away.
　　So Mrs. MacDuff, the cook, and he
　　Kept each other company.

Gregory Gray was six years old;
Eyes, sky blue—hair, red gold.
Quick as a chipmunk, wiry and thin,
Spattered with freckles from brow to chin.

He hadn't a soul with whom to play,
And he grew lonelier day by day.
In bed at every evening's end
    He would pretend
    He'd found a friend.

Late one night he watched the sight
Of a backyard, screeching, tomcat fight.
Savage, tough, they snarled and spat,
    Five
        Against one tiger cat.

With snap of jaw and swipe of paw,
The striped cat struck back, tooth and claw.
He was brave as a lion, Greg could tell,
So he gave him the name of Lionel.

The cook's window began to rattle.
Sleepy and cross, she stopped the battle,
Tossing out by ones and twos
Run-down slippers and shabby shoes.

Next day as Gregory sat at dinner,
He thought *No cat was ever thinner.*
He slithered silently from his chair
And set food on the outside stair—
    A bit of ham
    A riblet (lamb)
    Some sardines (two)
    A bit of stew
    Vienna sausages (a few).
He chased the cats who came to smell;
    This meal was just for Lionel.

Warily the Brave Beast came.
He ate, with jerks that shook his frame,
And ran when Gregory spoke his name.
"Gosh," sighed Gregory, "it's a shame
That Lionel is so hard to tame."

Each day Gregory put out food,
Choice leftovers, roasted, stewed.
    A pork leg slice
    Some Spanish rice
    A croquette (meat)
    Two crusts (whole wheat)
A fish head for a special treat.

Lionel gulped all that was brought,
Then fled before he could be caught.
Gregory worried at week's end—
Would Lionel *ever* be his friend?

"Lionel, no one's going to get you!
Look—I only want to pet you."
Lionel's eyes burned golden clear
As Gregory Gray came slowly near.
Gregory stirred.
What had he heard?
The wing of a bird
As it fluttered and whirred?

NO!
LIONEL PURRED!

Gregory stroked him. Joy complete!
Lionel rubbed against his feet.

"Mrs. MacDuff, may my friend come in, please?"
"That creature? Never! He's full of fleas!"
She swung her broom. "Scat! Go away!
He's not nice to play with, Gregory Gray."

Lionel had to hide.
Each night Gregory cried
As he slipped his scraps outside.
Now he was lonelier than before.
He couldn't see Lionel anymore,
Except for a peek at the kitchen door.

One day the cook said
"I've a pain in my head,
I'm going to bed.
There are books to be read
Or work puzzles instead.
If you get hungry, have jelly and bread.
Be a good boy, for I'm feeling half dead."

Greg gazed out at a circling sea gull;
The long afternoon was going to be dull.
Then he heard a sound he knew so well
On the back stairway—Lionel!
"I'll let you in, my Brave Beast. Come."
Lionel began to hum.
"We'll play it's meal time at the zoo."
Gregory gave him a bone to chew.

"What's going on?" cried a voice so gruff.
"I came down for my pills. . . "
  Mrs. MacDuff!
  Lionel streaked across the floor,
  The cook slam-banged the pantry door.
"He's trapped there. Good! I'll call the pound."
She twirled the phone dial round and round.

"Please, let's keep him!" Gregory pleaded.
"A home is what he's always needed.
I tamed him. Now he's not so tough."
"Nonsense, boy!" said Mrs. MacDuff.

"But—elephant, llama, pig, or moose,
   Every animal has some use."
   "That's enough!"
   Said Mrs. MacDuff.
"All alley cats can do is fight,
Keeping folks awake at night."

Inside the pantry something thumped,
Wrestled, tussled, rolled, and bumped;
Dishes clattered to the floor.
Gregory opened up the door.

Lionel marched proudly out.
Gregory gave a whooping shout.
   "Look! What do you think of that?
   My Brave Beast caught a rat!"

Lionel held up his prize.
The cook's two eyes grew round as pies.
"Rats in my pantry? Heavenly days!
Gregory Gray, your tomcat stays!
He must be well fed
And have a warm bed."

Gregory danced a jig and said,
  "He'll have his own dish
  With plenty of fish,
  The leftover chowder. . ."

"And flea-killing powder.
Now get rid of *that*!"
    The cook's voice grew louder.

As Gregory took away the rat,
Mrs. MacDuff gazed at the cat.
"You are just a scrawny, dumb thing.
Still. . . he's right.
    You're good for something."

"My aching head! A cup of tea
  Would be the very thing for me.
And I'll make for Gregory, in a minute,
Hot chocolate with marshmallows in it."
But first
  She fixed a soup-meat feast
For Lionel,
  Gregory Gray's Brave Beast.

ABOUT THE AUTHOR

Mary Collins Dunne lives in San Francisco with her husband and daughters. Although *Gregory Gray and the Brave Beast* is her first book with Childrens Press, she has had two books and many short stories published. She finds it thrilling to create characters, which become very real as she puts herself into the age, setting, and situation of her young main character and ponders what he would have done in particular circumstances. She enjoys many activities, including reading, gardening, sewing, swimming, and camping.

ABOUT THE ARTIST

Lois Axeman is a native Chicagoan who lives with her husband and two children in the city. After attending the American Academy and the Institute of Design (IIT), Lois started as a fashion illustrator in a department store. When the childrens wear illustrator became ill, Lois took her place and found she loved drawing children. She started free-lancing then, and has been doing text and picture books ever since.